Special Days

Poppy Day

Rosemary Moore

►Special Days◄

Bonfire Night
May Day
Mother's Day
Poppy Day

Editor: Carron Brown
Designer: Kate Buxton
Illustrator: David Antram
Cover illustrator: Barbara Loftus
Production controller: Carol Stevens

First published in 1997 by Wayland Publishers Limited,
61 Western Road, Hove, East Sussex, BN3 1JD

Find Wayland on the internet at http://www.wayland.co.uk

British Library Cataloguing in Publication Data

Moore, Rosemary 1928–
Poppy Day. – (Special Days)
1. World War, 1914–18 – Anniversaries, etc. – Juvenile literature
2. Remembrance Sunday – Great Britain – Juvenile literature
I. Title II.
940.4'6'0941

ISBN 0 7502 2042 2

Typeset by Kate Buxton, England
Printed and bound by G.Canale and C.S.p.A in Turin, Italy

Picture Acknowledgements
The publishers would like to thank the following for allowing us to reproduce their pictures: James Davis Travel Photography 15; Hulton Getty *cover*; Illustrated London News 10–11; Imperial War Museum 5, 7, 8; Popperfoto 4, 20; Rex Features *title page*, 21, 26, 27; Topham 28–9; Wayland Picture Library 14.

Contents

Poppies for remembrance

Every year, in November, we celebrate a special day. On this day, people wear a small red poppy, and they remember all the people who fought and died in the terrible wars of the twentieth century.

Over eighty years ago, the First World War was fought in Europe. Soldiers, sailors and airmen came from many countries of the world to take part.

▼ The poppy growing in the battlefields of France became the symbol of remembrance.

Thousands of people were killed in this war.
The poppies that we wear every November
are to remember their deaths and those of
many others who died in battle.

▼ British soldiers
resting before
going into battle.

1914 – war begins

In the summer of 1914, when your great-grandparents were young, a terrible war broke out between Britain and Germany.

To begin with, people on both sides wanted to take part. Many young men rushed to join the army. They thought the war would only last a few months. They were wrong. The war did not end until November 1918.

It seems strange to us now that people wanted to go away to fight in a war. But in those days, people felt strongly about fighting to protect their country and its ruler. In 1914, the king of Britain was the grandfather of our Queen Elizabeth II.

▲ Cheering soldiers going off to war.

War in the trenches

The young men who joined the army soon found that war was not as exciting as they had first thought. They were sent to France, where the British and German armies faced each other.

The soldiers had to shelter from the gunfire in deep, muddy trenches, with rats scurrying through them. They crouched, cold and hungry in the mud, while gunfire and shells roared overhead.

▲ Men had to live in the muddy trenches for many weeks.

Often the soldiers were ordered to leave the shelter of the trenches to attack the Germans with pistols and bayonets. Many soldiers were killed as soon as they left the trenches, shot by German gunfire.

'In Flanders Fields'

One of the men who went to war in France was a Canadian soldier, John McCrae. During a quiet moment in battle he wrote a poem called *In Flanders Fields*. Here is the first verse:

In Flanders fields the poppies blow
Between the crosses, row on row,
That mark our place: and in the sky
The larks, still bravely singing, fly
Scarce heard amid the guns below.

Later, John McCrae was badly wounded. He was taken to a hospital away from the battlefield, where he died.

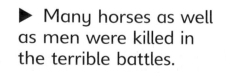
▶ Many horses as well as men were killed in the terrible battles.

Symbols of lost lives

At the end of the war an American called Moina Michael replied to McCrae's poem with a poem of her own. She called it *The Victory Emblem.* This is how her poem begins:

Oh! You who sleep in Flanders fields
Sleep sweet – to rise anew ...

The last verse tells people to wear a poppy.

And now the torch and Poppy red
Wear in honour of our dead ...

Moina and her friends bought poppies to wear. One friend had an idea: why not make paper poppies and sell them to help families of men who had died in the war?

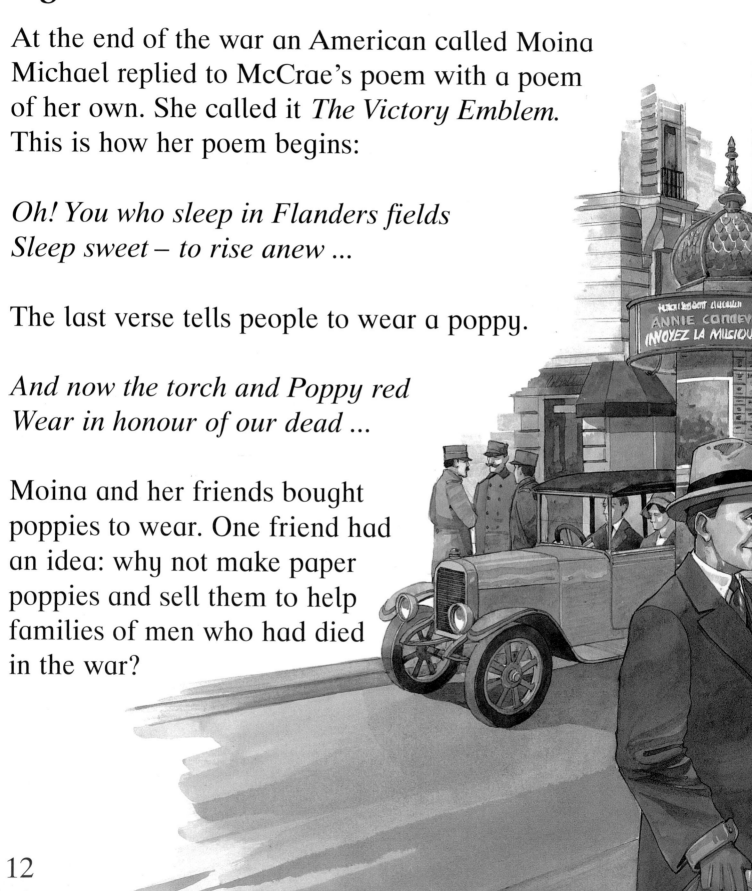

So, Poppy Day began. It was first held on
11 November 1921. The poppies were made
in France and sold to help children who lived
in places that were destroyed during the war.

Remembering those who died

After the war people felt very sad about all those who had died. They wanted to remember them in a special way, so they decided to build war memorials in their towns and villages. These were statues or stone crosses with the names of the soldiers, sailors and airmen killed in the war.

▶ Early in the war, soldiers who died were remembered with flowers and flags. Later, people wanted a special way to remember them.

14

In Britain, France and the USA, there are very special graves. These are graves to the 'Unknown Soldier'. No one knows who these soldiers were, but each died on the battlefields in northern France. A candle burns on these graves, in memory of all those who were killed.

◀ In London, a large war memorial, called the Cenotaph, was built. The Queen lays a wreath of poppies here every November.

1939 – back to war

Sadly, the peace that followed the end of the First World War did not stop a second terrible war. This time, German tanks rolled across France to the coast.

Soon, German planes started to bomb towns in Britain. British fighter planes attacked the big German bombers. Battles were fought at sea to protect the ships bringing food to Britain.

At last, in 1944, thousands of troops from Britain, the USA and other countries crossed the English Channel to France. After fierce fighting, the Germans were finally chased back to Germany.

▼ When the war broke out, some soldiers were left stranded in France. Sailors and fishermen crossed the English Channel in little ships to rescue them.

World-wide war

In 1945, the war against Germany was over. But there was still fierce fighting against Japan, who had joined the war on Germany's side. Troops from the USA, Britain, Australia, India and other countries fought the Japanese on Pacific islands and in Burma.

At last, the Japanese surrendered, after two of their cities were destroyed by atomic bombs.

Altogether, millions of people died during the Second World War. Besides those who fought in the war, thousands of children and their families were killed, injured or made homeless.

▶ In Burma, thousands of prisoners-of-war died building a railway for the Japanese in the jungle.

Remembrance Sunday

Since 1945, we remember all the people who died in the two world wars, and other wars fought all over the world. We remember them especially on the first Sunday in November, which is called Remembrance Sunday.

◀ A soldier who fought in the Second World War lays a remembrance cross among thousands placed outside Westminster Abbey.

▶ Poppy wreaths at the Cenotaph. Thousands of wreaths are laid at war memorials in towns and cities all over Britain on Remembrance Sunday.

Church services are held to honour those who died
in war, and wreaths of poppies are laid on war
memorials. People are silent for two minutes to
remember. At the Cenotaph in London, the Queen
and other important people attend a special
Remembrance Service and lay their poppy wreaths.

Men and women who fought in the wars, or helped
in other ways, such as nurses, ambulance drivers and
firefighters, march in front of the Cenotaph and lay
down their wreaths.

Making the poppies

All the poppies worn or used in wreaths on Poppy Day are made at the Poppy Factory in Richmond, near London. A hundred people work in the factory and another sixty make poppies in their homes.

The small poppies are made from paper with plastic stems. Bigger poppies, used in wreaths, are made from taffeta silk and have wire stems.

The money from the sale of the poppies is collected by an organization called the British Legion. The money is used to provide help and care for the families of people who fought in the wars.

▶ About forty million poppies are made at the poppy factory. Many are set in wreaths to be placed near memorials. Many others are sold on their own all over Britain.

Fifty years after

It is now more than fifty years since the Second World War ended. Your great-grandparents were probably children during the war. Were they evacuated to escape the bombing? Wherever they were during this time, they are sure to have interesting stories to tell.

In 1995, fifty years after the war ended, celebrations were held in London. Men and women who had served in the war marched past the Queen. Wartime bomber planes dropped millions of tiny poppies on the marching men and women.

▶ In 1995, millions of poppies rained down through the sky on to London.

The sadness of war

The Second World War ended in 1945, after the dropping of atomic bombs on Japan. Since then there have been no more 'world wars'.

But sadly, even though millions of people died in the two terrible world wars, there is still fighting in many parts of the world. Men, women and children still die, or are injured. Many are imprisoned or made homeless.

▼ These people have been made homeless by a recent war in their country.

The symbol of the poppy reminds us all of the uselessness of war and its waste of people's lives.

Glossary

Atomic bombs Very powerful bombs that can cause terrible destruction. Two were dropped on Japan at the end of the Second World War.

Bayonets Guns that have a sharp knife attached to the end for use during battle.

Emblem Something that people wear, like a poppy, to show they support and care about something.

Evacuated Sent away to a safe place to be protected from danger.

Flanders Part of the country of Belgium.

Honour To remember with pride what the men who fought in the war did.

Prisoners of war People who are captured during wartime by their enemy.

Servicemen The men who worked as soldiers, airmen and sailors in the wars.

Shells Metal cases filled with explosives that are fired from a large gun or cannon.

Surrender To give yourself up to an enemy.

Symbol An object that stands for something else.

Trenches Deep ditches dug for protection from gunfire during the First World War.

War memorials Monuments that were put up at the end of the First World War in memory of the people who died. They are now also for those who died in the Second World War and other wars in the twentieth century

Timeline

1914	1 August	The First World War begins.
1915		Colonel John McCrae writes *In Flanders Fields*.
1918		Moina Michael writes *The Victory Emblem*.
	9 November	She buys twenty-five red poppies, wearing one and selling the others to friends.
	11 November	Germany signs a peace treaty bringing the First World War to an end.
1919–20		Mme Guerin arranges for the sale of poppies to raise money to help ex-servicemen.
1920		The remains of an unknown British soldier killed in Flanders are buried in Westminster Abbey in a grave to the 'Unknown Soldier'.
1921		The British Legion is founded to provide help for people who had served in the armed forces.
1921	11 November	The first Poppy Day is held – the money raised from the sale of poppies is used to help children in towns and villages destroyed by war.
1922		The first Poppy Factory is set up in one small room.
1939	3 September	The Second World War begins.
1941		Japan enters the war on the side of Germany.
1944	6 June D-Day	The invasion against the German army in France begins.
1945	8 May	German troops surrender.
	6 and 7 August	An American plane drops atomic bombs on two Japanese cities.
	14 August	Japan surrenders.

Further information

Books to read
All About the First World War by Pam Robson (Macdonald Young Books, 1996)
War in the Trenches by Stewart Ross (Wayland, 1990)

For older readers:
Prisoners of War by Fiona Reynoldson (Wayland, 1990)
The Blitz by Fiona Reynoldson (Wayland, 1990)
Schools pack issued by the Royal British Legion Poppy Appeal
write to: Royal British Legion Village, Aylesford, Kent ME20 7NX

Places to visit
The Cenotaph, Whitehall, London
Or the war memorial in your local town or village.
If you visit these soon after Remembrance Sunday, you will see
all the poppy wreaths laid around the base of the memorial.

Coventry Cathedral, Coventry, Warwickshire
The bomb-destroyed remains of the ancient cathedral alongside
the splendid new cathedral are a symbol of the suffering endured
by British cities from German bombing.

HMS *Belfast* on the River Thames, London
This Second World War destroyer is also a floating museum.

Imperial War Museum, Kennington, London
This museum has many exhibitions about the two world wars,
and other warfare in the twentieth century.

Scottish National War Memorial, Edinburgh Castle, Edinburgh.

Westminster Abbey, London
Here you can see the grave to the 'Unknown Soldier'.

Index